Pugicorn
and the
Christmas Wish

Written by **Matilda Rose** • Illustrated by **Tim Budgen**

Hodder Children's Books

Rainbow
Lake

Twinkle
Castle

Coral Cove

If ever you find yourself in fairyland at Christmas time, make sure you pay a visit to the town of Twinkleton-Under-Beanstalk. Lights sparkle in every window, and Mrs Paws' Magic Pet Shop is filled with Christmas creatures – candy-cane kitties, snow-penguins and, of course, flying reindeer.

Ever since Princess Ava had collected
Pugicorn from The Magic Pet Shop,
she had been counting down the weeks
until his first Christmas.

"It's so exciting, Pugicorn! There'll be
presents and games and yummy treats –
and SNOW! Sparkling, shimmering snow!"

But this year, as Christmas drew nearer,
not a single flake of snow fell.

On Christmas Eve, the weather fairy gave
her final forecast. "I'm sorry everyone," she said,
"there will be no snow this Christmas."

Ava put on her bravest smile. "I'll still make sure you have the best first Christmas ever, Pugicorn."

Together, Ava and Pugicorn iced festive cookies,

they decorated their Christmas tree,

and they delivered a very special Christmas card.

Mrs Paws could tell they were sad about the snow. "Don't worry," she said with a wink. "Sometimes magical things happen at Christmas time . . ."

That night, Ava took one last hopeful peek out of the window. "I'm sorry your first Christmas won't be snowy, Pugicorn," she sighed as she climbed into bed.

But Pugicorn couldn't sleep. He knew how much Ava
wanted Christmas to be special. It just had to snow!

He scrunched up his eyes and made a very important Christmas wish . . .

Pugicorn opened one eye, then the other and – oh, tingly whiskers!
One . . . two . . . three snowflakes drifted past the window. Soon there
were too many to count, swirling and dancing through the air.

Pugicorn's wish had worked . . . it was snowing!

Pugicorn's excitement soon woke Ava.

"This is going to be the best Christmas
ever!" she cried, bursting with joy.
"Let's go and play, Pugicorn!"

They put on their boots and mittens and crept outside. Building snow-pugs and snow-princesses under the stars was even more magical than Ava had imagined!

Suddenly, Pugicorn heard a jingly noise above. He knew what *that* meant – Santa Claus! Ava had told him about Santa landing on rooftops to deliver presents all across fairyland.

But wait – Santa and his reindeer were
flying straight past Twinkleton!

"Oh no! The snow has covered everything
and Santa can't see the town!" Ava cried.

Pugicorn knew he had to do something, or there would
be no presents for anyone on Christmas morning.
But what could one little Pugicorn do?!

Pugicorn dashed off as quickly as his legs would carry him, flashing the light from his rainbow horn into the sky. But Santa kept on flying!

Pugicorn needed to get higher, and there was only one place tall enough . . .

. . . the Twinkleton Christmas tree!

Pugicorn looked up.
He felt a little bit funny.
Pugicorns are *not* natural
climbers . . . but we can all do
amazing things when we need to.

With his best friend cheering
him on, Pugicorn knew he
could be brave.

From the top of the tree, Pugicorn sent
a huge rainbow beam into the sky.

It worked! With a jingle of bells and a
loop-the-loop, Santa's sleigh whizzed back.

"Ho, ho, ho! Thank goodness for Pugicorn!" Santa chuckled.
"The most loyal pet in all of fairyland. Now, do you think
you and Ava could help me deliver these presents?"

The reindeer flew from roof to roof, with Pugicorn's glowing horn lighting up each chimney for Santa.

At last, all the presents were delivered. All except one . . .

"Make sure you don't open it until the morning," said Santa, handing Pugicorn his gift. "And thank you. You saved Christmas for all of Twinkleton!"

Then, with a jingling of bells and a "Merry Christmas!"
Santa and his reindeer took to the sky once more.

The next morning, Twinkleton woke to
the snowiest Christmas in fairyland history.

Princess Ava jumped out of bed, grinning with excitement.
She couldn't believe the night they'd had – this was already
the best Christmas ever and it was only just beginning!

Ava was thrilled with her presents. Santa knew JUST what she wanted, and Pugicorn seemed very happy with his gift too.

Ava and her friends tumbled out of their houses, laughing and playing in the snow.

It was the snowy Christmas they had all dreamed of. But for Ava, what made this year extra special was being able to spend it with the bravest pet in all of Twinkleton!

"Happy Christmas, Pugicorn," said Ava, and Pugicorn barked for joy.
Happy Christmas!

For Gabriella and Teddy
M.R.

For Annabelle, Alexander, Freya, Richard and Alina –
Happy Christmas!
T.B.

HODDER CHILDREN'S BOOKS

First published in Great Britain in 2020
by Hodder and Stoughton

© Hachette Children's Group, 2020
Illustrations by Tim Budgen

A CIP catalogue record for this book is available from the British Library.

PB ISBN: 978 1 44495 701 3

HB ISBN: 978 1 44495 876 8

1 3 5 7 9 10 8 6 4 2

Printed and bound in China

Hodder Children's Books
An imprint of Hachette Children's Group
Part of Hodder and Stoughton
Carmelite House, 50 Victoria Embankment, London, EC4Y 0DZ

An Hachette UK Company
www.hachette.co.uk
www.hachettechildrens.co.uk